D1430830

MICHAEL DAHL'S
REALLY SCARY STORIES

Michael Dahl's Really Scary Stories
are published by Stone Arch Books
A Capstone Imprint
1710 Roe Crest Drive
North Mankato, Minnesota 56003
www.mycapstone.com

Library of Congress Cataloging-in-Publication Data is available on
the Library of Congress website.

ISBN: 978-1-4965-3771-3 (library binding)
ISBN: 978-1-4965-3775-1 (ebook PDF)

Summary: When Dory opens up the mailbox to show the mailman her
pet monster, she finds that the mailbox is empty! Is Dory's monster
real, or part of her imagination? Find out what happens to Dory, the
mailman, and many others in this collection of spooky stories. And
watch out when opening your mailbox!

Designer: Hilary Wacholz
Image Credits: Dmitry Natashin

Printed in Canada.
032016   009647F16

THE MONSTER
IN THE MAILBOX
AND OTHER SCARY TALES

By Michael Dahl

Illustrated by
Xavier Bonet

STONE ARCH BOOKS
a capstone imprint

TABLE OF CONTENTS

The girl's face was pale. Her lips were blue as if she had been standing out in a blizzard. Her eyes were empty sockets.

The tiny creatures said nothing, but they filled the air with the grinding of their sharp, white teeth.

There was a low hum, and Arjun's father slumped over in his chair. The handheld device dropped from his grasp and slid onto the floor.

Dear Reader,

When I was young, there was an old, shadowy tree right outside my bedroom window. At night the shadows made weird, unsettling shapes, and I was convinced two blackbirds with sharp beaks were sitting on the branches, staring at me.

My mother had to pull down the window shade every night to help stop my nightmares.

I also thought there were bears living in my closet. And each night they tried to come out.

At the time, we lived across the alley from a funeral home. One afternoon, a man who worked there asked my father to help him unload a delivery from a truck. New coffins.

I guess I've always been around strange stuff. It's part of my blood, my brain, and my dreams.

And a few **NIGHTMARES** . . .

Michael Dahl

THE WRONG BUS

Lora stood at the bus stop and yawned. Another dull, gray morning. The rain clouds looked like they would burst any minute and soak her to the bone. Had her dad told her to take an umbrella? She couldn't remember.

It was only Wednesday, and Lora was dead tired.

She barely remembered getting out of bed, putting on her clothes, eating a toaster snack, grabbing her backpack, and heading out the door. She did it every day, without thinking. Somehow, with her eyes half open and her shoes untied, Lora lumbered across the busy street and waited for the bus.

Lora stood at the bus stop and listened to the morning sounds. People walking past. Kids talking to each other. Dogs barking. Car horns. A siren rushing off into the distance.

Lora looked up and down the street for the siren but didn't see it. Suddenly, the bus was right in front of her, its door open, waiting for her to climb on. She had been looking for the siren so intently that she missed hearing the bus squeak to a stop, like it did every morning. Lora sighed. She hiked her backpack onto her shoulder and trudged up the bus steps. She was looking down at her loose laces and the dirty floor when the bus driver startled her.

"Grab a seat, kid."

It was a new driver. His face was so full of wrinkles, she couldn't tell if he was smiling or not. *Hope the old guy can see the road,* Lora thought as the door shut with a loud screech. There was a rattle and a cough, and the bus pulled away from the curb.

Lora found the last empty seat. Not her regular one, but one near the back. The other girl sitting there did not slide over. She wanted to be on the aisle. She barely moved her knees so Lora could squeeze in and sit by the dirty window. Lora didn't recognize her.

Lora yawned again, then looked around. She didn't recognize any of the other students. Maybe she had missed her regular bus.

Lora turned toward the window, but the glass was coated with frost. Lora hadn't realized how cold it was. She cupped her hands together and blew on them. *The heater must be broken,* she thought. Lora put her fist on the glass and wiped at the frost. After a few moments, she could see green rolling hills and plenty of trees without leaves. Where were they? And how had they gotten out of the city so quickly?

She heard the girl next to her. "Don't worry. This is the right bus. We'll get there in time."

Lora turned. The girl's face was pale. Her lips were blue as if she had been standing out in a blizzard. Her eyes were empty sockets. Her mouth barely opened when she spoke. "We'll get there. The cemetery is only a few more miles."

"Cemetery?" croaked Lora. "I thought this was the school bus."

"It is," said the girl.

The bus lurched to a stop.

"Everybody out," cried the bus driver.

All the students stood up and shuffled down the aisle to the door. Lora was last. When she climbed off the bus, her shoes touched a dirt road instead of the school's black asphalt parking lot. Behind them stood a tall gate of black metal, with stone walls stretching on either side. In front was a wide green lawn dotted with fallen wet leaves. Among the leaves were several dozen tombstones, new and white. Lora watched as all the students walked.

The girl with the blue lips who had sat next to her walked up to a tombstone. When the girl reached it, she turned and looked back at Lora.

"You don't want to be late for school," she said. Then the girl slid down into the ground, as if she were standing on a trapdoor.

Lora watched as all of the students, each at a separate grave, were sucked into the grassy ground, one by one, until she was alone.

She turned. The bus was gone. The metal gates were closed behind her. Then she heard a familiar sound. A school bell was ringing somewhere. Somewhere deep underground.

THE POT
OF GOLD

"It's not a fairy," said Ari. "It's a leprechaun!"

"Quiet," said Essie. "My mom doesn't know I have him in here."

The two girls crowded next to the small glass jar that Essie was hiding in her closet.

"Look at his little cap," Ari said. "And his shoes. And his little jacket."

The tiny creature that sat inside the glass jar frowned at them. He stood up and shook his little fist. One of his shoes got stuck in a gooey glob. When he tried freeing himself, the little creature fell into a clump of dried grass. Ari and Essie tried not to laugh, but the man's frown grew wider and his green eyes glowered.

"I thought honey would be good for him to eat," Essie said. "I can dribble it through the air holes on top without taking off the lid."

"Where did you find him?" asked Ari.

"I was looking in the backyard for four-leaf clovers," Essie said, "and then I saw him."

"That proves he's a leprechaun," said Ari. "They like four-leaf clovers."

The little man was licking off the honey that had stuck to his shoe.

"Gross!" said Ari. The girls pointed and laughed. The leprechaun clapped his hands over his ears. His face wrinkled with pain.

"What's his problem?" said Ari.

"Maybe our laughter is too loud for him," said Essie.

Ari whispered, "Did you ask him about his pot of gold?"

"What's that?" said Essie.

Ari gasped. "You don't know? Every leprechaun guards a pot full of gold. And if you catch one, they have to tell you where it is!"

The two girls looked at each other and then stared at the tiny man in green. He was sitting down in the grass, his back turned to them. His shoulders were shaking.

"Where's your pot of gold?" Ari asked, as loudly as she dared. The little man did not move.

"You ask him," said Ari. "You're the one who caught him."

"Where's your gold?" Essie asked. "I want it."

He turned slowly and looked at them over his shoulder. He nodded sadly. "Very well," he said in a buzzing voice. "You have won my treasure."

The girls squealed in delight.

"Where is it?" asked Ari.

The man pointed a little finger at Essie. "Take me outside, and I shall lead you there," he said.

The two girls stepped out into the backyard where moonlight had turned the grass into a silvery carpet. Essie pulled the jar out of her hoodie pocket and held it up to her face. "Now where?" she asked. The little man pointed away from the house and down the street.

"Remember," said Ari, "we split it half and half. I was the one who told you about the gold, otherwise you'd never have known about it."

"Okay, okay," said Essie. "Half and half."

It was an hour later when the girls entered a wooded area far from their neighborhood.

"This is taking too long," said Ari. "Tell him to hurry up or we're going home."

"And forget about the gold?" asked Essie.

Ari's voice was tired. "If we don't find that pot soon, tell him we're going to smash the jar against a tree."

Essie gasped. She was shocked by Ari's suggestion, but she didn't say anything. She wanted that gold.

The glass jar buzzed. The leprechaun was jumping up and down. "Behold, behold," the tiny creature kept repeating.

Blinding color swirled around the girls. Waves of brilliant light, blue and green and purple and red, poured onto Ari and Essie like sheets of rain. "The rainbow!" cried Ari. "A leprechaun's pot of gold is always at the end of a rainbow!"

"I love rainbows!" Essie shouted, laughing.

The ground beneath the girls' feet shivered. A brilliant, golden glow streamed upward through cracks in the ground. The cracks grew wider and wider. Suddenly the golden light went out. Ari and Essie saw a giant metal pot, as large as a swimming pool, resting in a crater at their feet. It was turning from gold to gray.

"Let me out," buzzed the leprechaun, "or the gold is gone!"

Essie placed the jar on the ground and quickly unscrewed the lid. The leprechaun leaped out. He took a deep breath and smiled. He raised his little arms and shouted. Before they knew what was happening, the girls were surrounded by thousands of little green men, falling out of the trees, crawling out from under leaves. The tiny creatures said nothing, but they filled the air with the grinding of their sharp, white teeth.

Essie and Ari screamed. They backed away from the swarm of leprechauns. They lost their footing and tumbled into the massive pot, sliding down the smooth metal side until they landed in a heap at the bottom.

"Where's the gold?" asked Essie.

The two friends looked around. The metal had now turned to a dull black.

"You must work for it!" yelled the leprechaun from far above. He stood on the brim a hundred feet above them. He threw some fluttery objects into the air. When they landed at the girls' feet, Ari recognized the objects as dirty rags.

"Let us out!" shouted Ari. She knew it would be impossible to climb the steep, slippery metal.

"I shall, dear lass," said the leprechaun. "As soon as you two polish the pot and turn it back into gold."

The girls looked down at the skimpy rags. "But that will take forever!" wailed Essie.

"Not forever," giggled the leprechaun. "Only a hundred years."

The leprechauns gathered around the edge of the crater, looking down at their victims. The girls clapped their hands over their ears as a horrible, loud and grating roar echoed throughout the massive pot. Ari was certain that what they were hearing was the sound of leprechaun laughter.

THE DRAIN

Arjun hated drains. He couldn't watch the soapy water flowing past his bare feet and swirling into the shower drain. If things went *down* a drain, that meant that things could also come *up*. Anything.

A flash of lightning lit up the bathroom and shower stall. Then darkness.

"This is just great!" Arjun said aloud to himself. "Just great!"

He carefully climbed out of the shower, feeling his way through utter darkness to the towel rack. "That's all we need," he said. "Another power outage!"

Arjun dried off, got dressed, and then groped his way into the living room where he found his father hunched over a glowing blue light.

"Dad, how can you still be playing games?" he asked. "There's a storm outside and the power's out. It's all over the neighborhood. No lights. Nothing."

"Huh, that's cool," his dad mumbled without taking his eyes off his handheld device.

Arjun was always worried about losing power. Everything in his world — everything important that is — relied on a constant supply of power. How could he live without batteries, chargers, wall outlets, or wireless Internet?

The boy walked over behind his dad.

"Uh, oh. Look at your battery icon," Arjun said, peering over his dad's right shoulder. "You're running on reserves and they're almost gone." From where he stood, he could see the blue screen of the handheld device.

His dad never took his eyes off the glowing screen in his hands. "It's fine, Ari," he said. "No worries. I'll be able to finish this game long before —"

His dad stopped talking. There was a low hum, and Arjun's father slumped over in his chair. The handheld device dropped from his grasp and slid onto the floor.

He looked once more at the battery indicator built into his dad's back.

No power.

"Great!" said Arjun, rolling his eyes. "Another power drain." Arjun hated drains.

Maybe having a robot father is just too much work, he thought. Maybe he should ask for a refund.

I ONLY SEE CHOCOLATE

"I love, love, love chocolate!" exclaimed Sara.

She and her friends Holly and Aruna were standing outside the new bakery. Bright June sunshine shone on the front window and freshly painted golden letters read:

ORBWICH SISTERS BAKED GOODS & SWEETS

A sign on the door announced:

Opening Day!

"Look at that éclair!" Aruna pointed.

"That can't be an éclair," said Holly. "It's too big."

"I know," replied Aruna, smiling. "Yum!"

Sara had her eye on a double-decker cake stand covered with dozens of small, dark globes. "Chocolate-covered cherries," read the sign. *My absolute favorite,* thought Sara.

"Who's going in first?" asked Holly. "I want to see Aruna eat that monster éclair!"

The bakery had been an empty storefront just the day before. Now it stood like a shiny gingerbread house, with candy-colored decorations and a bright yellow door. Sara pushed it open, making a bell jingle sweetly as she and her friends stepped inside.

A dozen customers were already there, browsing through shelves and tables and cases. The tiny store was filled with breads, cakes and cupcakes, cookies, donuts, and — Sara spied them at once — chocolate-covered cherries.

"Red velvet cupcakes!" said Holly.

"This place smells like my grandma's cookie jar!" said Aruna.

Sara left her friends staring at goodies while she walked toward the big glass cases at the back of the store. Two women stood behind the cases and handed customers their chosen sweets from the loaded shelves. A third woman stood at the cash register ringing up bags full of baked goods. They each wore a gleaming white apron, a soft white chef's cap, and a pair of dark sunglasses.

That's rude, thought Sara. Sara's mother had taught her it was impolite to wear sunglasses indoors.

One of the women behind the case turned toward Sara. "Can I help you, young lady?" she asked.

Next to the woman's mouth was a large mole with three hairs growing out of it. Sara tried hard not to stare at it.

"There are other customers waiting behind you," said the woman gently.

"Oh, sorry," said Sara. "I'll have five chocolate-covered cherries."

"Excellent choice," said the woman. "My favorite."

"Mine too!" echoed Sara.

The woman dropped five of the chocolate globes into a crisp white bag. "I'll tell you a secret," she whispered, handing the bag over the counter. "These taste better when they're eaten fresh."

The girl felt the warmth of the chocolate through the crisp paper. She smelled the thick, sweet scent, and her mouth watered.

"Sara!" Aruna bumped into her with a giggle. "Guess what? I got *two* éclairs! And I don't care how big they are."

Holly joined them. She was holding a bag bigger than either of theirs. "Cupcakes," she explained. "For my family."

The woman at the register took Sara's money and handed back her change. She smiled widely. Her teeth looked like little sugar cubes.

The bell over the door jingled again as the girls stepped outside. They walked together quietly for several minutes, each girl absorbed in eating her own special treat.

Sara had chewed three of the delicious chocolate-covered cherries when she asked, "Where do you think they came from?"

"The cherries?" asked Aruna.

"No, I mean those ladies. They looked sort of weird to me," said Sara.

"And what's with the sunglasses?" said Holly.

"I know!" said Sara.

"Who cares?" asked Aruna. "Their treats are delicious." She stuffed the rest of a dripping éclair into her already-full mouth.

Holly and Sara nodded in agreement.

A few quiet minutes passed. Sara had another chocolate-covered cherry. "But I mean, like, the bakery wasn't even there yesterday," Sara said. "No signs or anything."

"My mother said there was nothing in the newspaper, either," said Holly. Her family lived across the street from the new bakery. Her mother had seen the store just that morning and told Holly about it. And Holly had called her friends.

"And how would they have time to bake everything?" asked Sara.

"They'd need tons of butter and sugar and

chocolate and stuff," added Holly. "But there were no cars or trucks around."

Aruna giggled. "Maybe they're witches," she said. Then she whispered, "Did you see the hairy mole on that one behind the counter?"

"So they just waved a wand and made everything magically appear?" said Holly.

The hot June sun warmed the girls' hands and faces. Sara reached for another cherry. The chocolates had started melting in the bag, and when she pulled out the next one, some of the chocolate had dripped away, revealing the bright red cherry underneath.

Sara looked closer. It wasn't a cherry.

It was an eye.

A human eye.

THE RACK

Walter saw things out of the corners of his eyes. His older brother sneaking up to scare him, for instance. His science teacher, Mr. Hayes, walking toward his desk when Walter was reading the latest Iron Man comic. Annoying runners on the sidewalk when he was walking to the comic book store. These were all things it was helpful to see, to know in advance, so he could prepare himself. Turn to yell at his brother. Hide Iron Man under his science book. Step aside so the huffing, puffing runner wouldn't knock him over.

But Walter saw other things too. Things he couldn't always explain. Not at first.

Once, he thought he saw an ogre-like being squatting in the corner of his grandmother's living room. He turned and saw that it was just a fancy, old-fashioned chair with a quilt draped over it. At the grocery store he was sure he saw a tall werewolf peering over his shoulder. It turned out to be a large cardboard cutout of a cartoon character for cereal.

"Walter, you're so stupid," he told himself. "Calm down and take a look before you think an alien from another planet is going to attack you or something."

Walter's family lived in a small, crowded house, so there were lots of weird shapes he saw from the corners of his eyes. It always turned out to be a shadow, or light from a car outside a window, or wind blowing the curtains. Or his cat, Fido.

The shape that bothered him most was the coatrack in the back hallway. It stood seven feet tall and was made out of dark wood with six claw feet. At the top were six short branches, where anyone could hang a coat or hat or scarf. Every time Walter walked past the hallway, even though he knew it was the same old coatrack, he thought he saw a man standing there. Out of the corner of his eye he saw a tall, skinny man without a face. Of course he didn't have a face, Walter told himself. There was no face. It was just his dad's hat. A long coat had suggested a tall, slender body. All the same, Walter never walked down that hallway at night.

One afternoon, he came home after school and the house felt empty. Again, like a hundred other times, he saw the skinny man out of the corner of his eye. Tall and slender. Long dark arms scraping against the floor. No face. This time, however, Walter was prepared.

"Don't be so dramatic," he whispered to himself. "Don't freak out. It's the same dumb coatrack that's always there." Walter refused to turn and look at the coatrack, proving to himself that he was not stupid. Not afraid.

Walter heard a noise. He had thought the house was empty.

"Is that you, honey?" came his mother's voice from somewhere upstairs.

Walter felt the tension melt away from his shoulders. "Yeah, I'm home," he replied.

"I've been busy cleaning all day," said his

mother. "So don't walk on the kitchen floor until it's dry."

"Okay, Mom."

"And if you're wondering where that old coatrack is," she added, "I moved it out of the back hallway. It's by the front door now."

Walter felt as if he had fallen into a pool of ice-cold water.

There was no coatrack in the hallway.

He couldn't move. He couldn't make himself turn around to look.

Something behind him cleared its throat. Then he heard the sound of knuckles scraping against the floor.

SOMETHING'S WRONG WITH LOCKER 307

Dear Principal Pirelli,

My name is Jeremy Hawke. I am a student here at Lovecraft Middle School, and I have to warn you about something really bad. There's something wrong with locker 307. My locker is number 306. It is perfectly okay except for the dried gum on the inside door that I can't get rid of. And the hinges squeak. But locker 307 is dangerous. Really and truly dangerous. I know that sounds crazy. I would come tell you in person, but I thought it would be better to write all this down in case I forgot anything important.

Don't let any kid use that locker. Please!!!!

You probably have a computer report somewhere about all the lockers and all the kids who used them over the years. Well, look up whoever was assigned locker 307. It's in the newer section of school. Do you notice anything weird?

This fall, the kid who had that locker next to mine, 307, was Haruki Mizo. We call him Rookie. I mean, we used to, when he was still here.

The second week of school I noticed that he carried all of his books around all the time. One day in the library, we were working on a geography project together. I asked him, "Why don't you leave some of your books in your locker?" He shook his head and didn't say anything.

Then I said, "Is it broken? Sometimes the lockers get broken and the custodians don't even know it."

"It opens," said Haruki. His voice sounded funny, like he was far away.

Then he got up from the table and walked out of the library. We were supposed to be partners, but he just walked away. Didn't say another word. I thought maybe he was sick. He looked sort of pale.

We didn't talk about the locker again until about a week ago. School was over, and I had stayed late for the Science Fiction and Manga Club meeting. I was at my locker, getting my geography book for homework and slipping it into my backpack, when I heard something inside Haruki's locker. It sounded like a baby crying. I walked closer to his locker and put my ear up by the vents. The noise was clearer and louder. It didn't sound like a baby anymore, but like an animal howling in the distance.

I looked around to see if anyone else nearby could hear it. The halls were empty. Then I spied Haruki standing at the end of the row of lockers.

"What's in there?" I asked.

A bang from the locker startled me. A deep growl came through the locker vents. Then another bang. Something on the other side of the door was trying to get out.

I dropped my backpack and ran over to

Haruki. "We have to tell someone," I said. "We have to tell the principal."

"No," he said. "No, I can't." At first, I thought he was going to cry. Then he said, "I'm sorry."

"What are you talking about?" I said.

"I'm sorry you know about the locker," he said. Then his eyes got all cold and creepy, like he was a robot or something. He stared and stared. "You heard it, didn't you?" he said. "It's too late now. You heard it."

The locker door rattled.

Haruki looked at the locker. "It won't get out," he said quietly. "It doesn't need to."

"What is going on?" I was practically shouting at him.

"You know the kid who had that locker before me?" he asked.

I didn't.

"Her name was Alice Johnson," he said.

"You mean Weird Alice?" I said. "I remember her. She moved last year, right before summer vacation."

"She didn't move," Haruki said. "She disappeared. So did her family."

Haruki was creeping me out. "How do you know that?"

"I heard the story from one of Alice's friends after she disappeared," said Haruki. "When I was assigned Alice's locker, number 307, Denise Gonzales told me that Alice was afraid of it."

My stomach turned to ice. Denise Gonzales was a girl from our grade. She had left school earlier this year. No one heard why she left. There were all kinds of rumors — that her parents were spies, that they were wanted by the police. The one thing we knew for certain was that she was gone, and so was her family.

"Anyone who has that locker," said Haruki, "or hears about what it does . . . they . . . they . . ."

"They what?" I shouted.

"They disappear," said Haruki.

This was getting stupid. Now I was mad. "Lockers don't do anything." I looked back at locker 307. "There's just something wrong with it. Maybe there's a squirrel trapped inside or something."

Haruki looked up at me. "Did that sound like a squirrel to you?" he asked.

"It could be a big squirrel," I said.

Haruki started walking away. "Hey!" I shouted. "What do you mean? How do you know it's not a squirrel?"

Haruki shook his head. "Just get away," he said. Then he ran down the hall toward the front doors.

Locker 307 was quiet now. I stood there for a while, not moving, hardly even breathing. Just listening. The noises had stopped.

I tiptoed back toward my own locker and picked up my backpack. Then I quietly shut my locker door, spun the dial, and backed away.

I heard something.

"Who's there?" I yelled. "Haruki, is that you?"

A soft growl came from locker 307. The growl turned into a husky voice and said, "I'll see you later."

I ran down the hall. When I reached the front door of the school, I heard a metallic sound behind me. It sounded horrible, like a locker door being ripped apart. Then I ran home fast, not daring to look back. I wanted to tell my parents about it, but then I thought about what Haruki had said. Anyone who has the locker or hears about what it does disappears. I thought about Alice Johnson and Denise Gonzales and their families.

Then I thought about how crazy it all seemed. I wondered if it could have been a trick. Haruki was really smart, after all. Maybe he'd worked up this trick, using sound effects or something.

But the next day, Haruki didn't show up at school. The day after that, our teacher stood up and made an announcement. Mrs. Langston said that Haruki Mizo and his family had moved away. He would not be at school anymore.

I didn't use my locker that day. Or the next. I told my teachers I had lost my books so they would give me new ones. I carried them around with me all day. I didn't even walk down the hall where my locker was.

Because I know what happened to Haruki and Alice and Denise, and I know it could happen to me too. That's why I'm writing this all down, Mr. Pirelli. So I can give it to you tomorrow morning as soon as school starts. So you can keep other kids safe from locker 307.

– Jeremy Hawke

The following pages were discovered in a backpack that was found on the grounds of Lovecraft Middle School by Mr. Matthew Jackson, one of the school's custodians. The backpack belonged to a former student, Jeremy Hawke. The Hawke family moved suddenly out of the area shortly after the beginning of the school year, without notifying the school. Strangely, all of the Hawke family's furniture and belongings were left in their house. None of Jeremy's friends have heard from him since.

After these papers were discovered, the custodian, Mr. Jackson, gave them to the principal, Anthony Pirelli. It has been one week, and no one has seen Mr. Jackson or Mr. Pirelli. An investigation is under way.

THE
MONSTER
IN THE
MAILBOX

Mr. Howard Finn, the neighborhood's new mailman, had never met anyone like Dory before. The little girl never stopped talking.

"This one's Mrs. Gomez's house. She has twelve grandchildren. Twelve's a lot, isn't it? She must get a lot of presents for her birthday. I like presents. Especially games and puzzles. But I don't want grandchildren. I wonder what kind of presents Mrs. Gomez gets."

Dory was eight years old with pumpkin-colored hair. Mr. Finn had met her as soon as he stepped out of his mail truck. He was hauling the heavy mailbag over his shoulder when Dory appeared at his side. She told him she would help him because this was his first day.

"It's not my first day delivering the mail," Mr. Finn had pointed out. "But it is my first day in your neighborhood."

"My family just moved in a few weeks ago, so I know what it feels like," Dory said.

Mr. Finn had dropped off mail, and a few packages, to four of the neighborhood homes when he asked about Dory's house. The little girl frowned and pointed across the street.

"That's a big house," said Mr. Finn. Four stories of glass and steel towered above the nearby houses. No trees or bushes or flowers grew in the yard. Instead, there were a dozen boulders — big boulders — scattered across a field of white gravel. Mr. Finn thought it looked more like a machine than a house. No wonder the little girl was frowning.

Mr. Finn kept talking while he dug into his bag for the next customer's mail. He didn't want to let go of his end of the conversation, or Dory might start chattering again.

"Do you have any brothers or sisters?" he asked.

Dory shook her head. "Not really," she said.

Mr. Finn thought that was an odd answer.

Dory added, "But I have a pet —"

"Oh, that's nice," the man said. "I always liked pets when I was a boy. Dog or cat?"

Dory shook her head again.

"A hamster, maybe?" asked Mr. Finn.

"It's a monster," said Dory, smiling.

"Oh, I see," said Mr. Finn. This little girl really was odd. "A monster, huh? Is he a nice monster?"

"It's a girl monster," said Dory. "She's very nice. But sometimes she gets very, very hungry."

Mr. Finn walked across Mrs. Gomez's yard and up the front steps of her house. He slipped the mail through a slot in the door, and then started toward the next house, the Hendersons'. The last one on that block. "So do you let your monster play in the yard?" asked Mr. Finn.

"She's not allowed outside," said Dory. "That makes her very sad."

"So where do you keep her?" the man asked while digging into his mailbag again.

"She's in the mailbox."

Mr. Finn stopped digging and looked down at the girl. Dory was busy pulling clovers from the Hendersons' lawn. "Ten, eleven, twelve," she counted. The man glanced across the street at her house, the glass-and-steel giant. After this block, Dory's house was next on his route.

Then he saw the mailbox. It looked ordinary, a small metal box sitting atop a post. It stood at the bottom of concrete steps that led up to Dory's front yard with the boulders and the white gravel.

"She lives in the mailbox?" repeated Mr. Finn. "She must be a little monster, then."

"Nuh-uh," said Dory. "She's big."

Mr. Finn walked slowly across the Hendersons' yard to the next-door house, never taking his eyes off of the mailbox across the street. "If she's so big, how does she fit in there?" he asked quietly.

Dory giggled. "She's all squishy and squashy," said the little girl. "I just push her really hard and she pops right in."

Mr. Finn had decided that Dory was clearly strange. But she also had a big imagination. *Typical lonely, bright child,* he thought. Like he had been as a boy. *Probably doesn't have any friends in the neighborhood yet,* he told himself. *Which is why she's following me.*

He dropped the mail at the last house on the block and then slowly started across the street.

"Yay!" said Dory. Then she sang, "We're going to my house!"

Mr. Finn looked at her mailbox again. Squishy, squashy. And didn't the kid say her pet was very, very hungry? Or was he just making that up?

The man reached into his bag and pulled out the few envelopes that were addressed to Dory's house. He held them out to the little girl. "Here," he said, trying to smile. "You can give them to your parents."

"Oh, no," said Dory. "I'm not supposed to touch the mail. Daddy says it's too important. It has to go in the mailbox."

Mr. Finn licked his lips. "But it's only a few —"

"No!" said Dory. She stamped her foot. "It has to go in the mailbox."

Mr. Finn straightened his back. He held his head up. *I'm a grown man,* he told himself. *This is ridiculous, to be frightened by some little girl's story.* He stepped closer to the mailbox. Dory stepped aside to give him more room. Her eyes grew wide. She even stopped talking.

The mailman reached out with both hands. One held the letters, the other gripped the metal tab on top of the mailbox door.

He took a deep breath.

"Nooooo!" wailed Dory. "She's gone!"

Mr. Finn opened his eyes. He hadn't even realized he had closed them. He didn't remember opening the mailbox. But the door was open and the inside was as normal as every other one he'd seen. An ordinary metal box. That's all it was.

"Where did she go?" cried Dory.

Mr. Finn felt sorry for the girl. "Maybe she was feeling too squished in there," he said. "Maybe she's looking for another mailbox."

"But she liked *this* mailbox!" said Dory.

Mr. Finn walked back to his truck. Over his shoulder, he waved to Dory and called out, "See you tomorrow."

Dory was frowning but she still waved. "Tomorrow," she mumbled. Then she turned and started trudging up the concrete steps to her front yard.

The little girl heard a scream. It came from the mail truck. The truck was rocking back and forth. She could see through the windows on the side that seven long, black tentacles, covered in blood-red suckers, were twisting and thrashing inside. She spotted Mr. Finn's white face pressed up against the glass, then he was gone.

Dory sighed happily. Maybe the nice mailman was right. Maybe her pet was getting a little too big for the mailbox.

ABOUT THE AUTHOR

Michael Dahl, the author of the Library of Doom and Troll Hunters series, is an expert on fear. He is afraid of heights (but he still flies). He is afraid of small, enclosed spaces (but his house is crammed with over 3,000 books). He is afraid of ghosts (but that same house is haunted). He hopes that by writing about fear, he will eventually be able to overcome his own. So far it is not working. But he is afraid to stop. He claims that, if he had to, he would travel to Mount Doom in order to toss in a dangerous piece of jewelry. Even though he is afraid of volcanoes. And jewelry.

ABOUT THE ILLUSTRATOR

Xavier Bonet is an illustrator and comic-book artist who resides in Barcelona. Experienced in 2D illustration, he has worked as an animator and a background artist for several different production companies. He aims to create works full of color, texture, and sensation, using both traditional and digital tools. His work in children's literature is inspired by magic and fantasy as well as his passion for the art.

MICHAEL DAHL TELLS ALL

When you wake up each morning, have you ever found a stack of papers next to your bed that contain everything you will say that day, and everything that will be said to you? Me neither. Instead, conversations are built from listening to people, thinking about what they've said, and then responding. Back and forth it goes. Listen, think, respond, repeat. I try to listen to the world around me: to friends, strangers, books, comics, podcasts, TV shows, songs. What do they remind me of? What if those things happened to me? What if I changed the words in a song or a scene in a movie? New ideas start piling up in an imaginary stack of papers in my brain. Here's where I got the ideas for the stories in this book.

THE WRONG BUS

I once took the wrong bus, but I didn't end up where Lora does in the story. It was an after-school bus and I wasn't paying attention to the bus numbers. I was so used to hopping on the bus at the front of the line that I never considered the buses might sometimes be in a different order. I ended up way, way past my house and neighborhood. It was a scary experience for a kid. Especially someone like me who scares easily.

THE POT OF GOLD

For Christmas one year, my sister Linda gave me an unusual gift. It was a small six-sided jar with a lid screwed on top. Inside was a tiny ceramic figure of a boy fairy, eyes wide, his hands over his mouth, trapped. I loved that present! I must have smiled at it a hundred times over the years. Recently, I gave it a glance, and I could swear the little creature moved. It might have been just a glimmer of sunshine bouncing off the glass. Whatever it was, it gave me the seed for the story.

THE DRAIN

My good friend and fellow author, Donnie Lemke, gave me the idea for this little tale. I told him that I was compiling a list of things that scare me or other people I know. My sister Linda is afraid of drains.

And snakes. She's especially afraid of a snake coming out of a drain! When Donnie heard me say the word "drain," he thought of a completely different kind of drain. What if there was a storm, he asked, and the power was draining away, and . . . the story was right there!

I ONLY SEE CHOCOLATE

My father loved chocolate-covered cherries. My sister would always buy him a box of them for Christmas, a present he looked forward to each year. And each Christmas morning, he'd sit there eating his chocolates, while the rest of us opened our gifts. I, however, never liked cherries. Today, if I order a chocolate malt and it comes with a cherry on top — yeek! I either give it to someone else or fling it out the window and onto the grass. It's organic. It's good for the grass.

THE RACK

In the house where I grew up in north Minneapolis, my parents had a strange bedroom. The closets, at one end of the room, didn't have doors. They were always open. And when, as a child of four, I would sometimes slip into my parents' bed at night because I was scared by a bad dream, or by the imaginary birds outside my window, I would see those open closets. The clothes hanging there looked like people standing and watching me. I couldn't decide which was worse: going back to my own bedroom with the birds, or staying in my parents' room with the shadowy clothes-people. I did not sleep a lot in that house.

SOMETHING'S WRONG WITH LOCKER 307

This story did not come easily. It went through several re-writes. I knew I wanted to write about a letter found in a locker, a letter explaining something horrible and mysterious that had happened to a student, but I just wasn't getting it right. After two of my editors read it and gave me their feedback, the story turned into one about the actual locker itself. That's why you have editors. They help make your stories better — or in this case, spookier.

THE MONSTER IN THE MAILBOX

Lots of writers make up stories to answer a question they have. The question that buzzed inside my head one afternoon was, "Where is the least likely place to find a monster?" I came up with various answers: a spray bottle of cheese, a car's glove compartment, a balloon, a birdhouse. Later in the day, I was checking my mailbox, and that's when I discovered the perfect hiding spot — a place people visit every day without even thinking about it.

GLOSSARY

aisle (ILE) — the passage that runs between two rows of seats

boulders (BOHL-durs) — large, rounded rocks

cemetery (SEM-i-ter-ee) — a place where dead people are buried

crater (KRAY-tur) — a large hole in the ground caused by something falling or exploding

customers (KUS-tuh-murs) — people who buy things from a store or business

device (di-VISE) — a piece of equipment that does a particular job

dribble (DRIB-uhl) — to drop liquid in small amounts

éclair (ih-KLAIR) — a small pastry filled with cream and topped with chocolate icing

lass (LAS) — a girl or young woman

leprechaun (LEP-ri-kahn) — a playful, annoying elf in Irish folklore who promises gold if you can catch him

outage (OUT-ij) — a period of time when a power supply is not available

tension (TEN-shuhn) — a feeling of nervousness that makes it difficult to relax

tentacles (TEN-tuh-kuhls) — long, flexible limbs of some animals such as octopuses and squid

wireless (WIRE-lis) — not requiring wires to work properly

DISCUSSION QUESTIONS

1. In the story "Something's Wrong With Locker 307," Jeremy is terrified of his friend Haruki's locker. Do you think you would've been scared of the locker? Discuss why or why not using examples from the text.

2. In "The Rack," Walter isn't sure whether or not he is imagining that the coatrack in his hallway is a person. Have you ever been spooked by something in your home or school? Talk about what it was and why it was scary.

3. What are some of your biggest fears? How could you make them into a spooky story? Discuss the possibilities, and then try writing one!

WRITING PROMPTS

1. Chocolate is Sara's absolute favorite food — until she finds out that the chocolate she's eating is covering up something really spooky and gross! Write a paragraph or two explaining where you think the eyeballs came from in the story "I Only See Chocolate," using examples from the text.

2. Imagine you are the bus driver in the story "The Wrong Bus." Write a version of the short story from his point of view.

3. A lot of scary stories involve monsters, like "The Monster in the Mailbox." Write a poem about Dory's monster, describing what you imagine it looks like.

MICHAEL DAHL'S
REALLY SCARY STORIES